STILL A GORILLA!

By **Kim Norman**
Illustrated by **Chad Geran**

Orchard Books • New York
An Imprint of Scholastic Inc.

Library of Congress Cataloging-in-Publication Data
Norman, Kim, author. • Still a gorilla! / by Kim Norman ; illustrated by Chad Geran.—First edition. pages cm
Summary: Willy the Gorilla imitates the other animals at the zoo, but despite pretending he remains always a gorilla.
ISBN 978-0-545-75791-1
1. Gorilla—Juvenile fiction. 2. Zoo animals—Juvenile fiction. 3. Identity (Psychology)—Juvenile fiction. 4. Stories in rhyme.
[1. Stories in rhyme. 2. Gorilla—Fiction. 3. Zoo animals—Fiction. 4. Self-acceptance—Fiction.]
I. Geran, Chad, illustrator. II. Title. • PZ8.3.N7498St 2016
[E]—dc23 • 2015027274
10 9 8 7 6 5 4 3 2   16 17 18 19 20

Printed in Malaysia 108
First edition, August 2016

Book design by Steve Ponzo

CITY ZOO

This is Willy.

Willy would like to be something else.

Maybe a lion?

If Willy strides outside and roars with pride, will Willy be a lion?

Will he?

No.
Still a gorilla!

What about a walrus?

If Willy's teeth grow wrong
(a foot too long!),
will Willy be a walrus?

Will he?

How about a billy goat?

If Willy chews on crates
or head butts gates,
will Willy be a billy goat?

Will he?

Perhaps an alligator?

If Willy creeps and chomps
in slimy swamps,
will Willy be an alligator?

Will he?

No.
Still a gorilla!

Maybe a
kangaroo?

If Willy thumps and jumps over plum-tree stumps, will Willy be a kangaroo?

Will he?

Well, how about this?
What if Willy

roars and grows,

chews and butts,

Yes!

Willy will be silly.
Very silly and . . .